SOPHIE the AWESOME

Finding the right name isn't easy!
See what else Sophie tries out. . . .

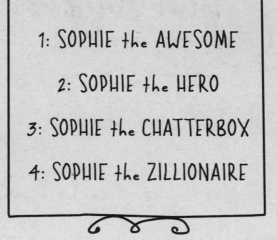

1: SOPHIE the AWESOME

2: SOPHIE the HERO

3: SOPHIE the CHATTERBOX

4: SOPHIE the ZILLIONAIRE

SOPHIE the AWESOME

by Lara Bergen

illustrated by Laura Tallardy

SCHOLASTIC INC.

New York Toronto London Auckland
Sydney Mexico City New Delhi Hong Kong

No part of this publication may be reproduced, stored in a retrieval system, or transmitted in any form or by any means, electronic, mechanical, photocopying, recording, or otherwise, without written permission of the publisher. For information regarding permission, write to Scholastic Inc., Attention: Permissions Department, 557 Broadway, New York, NY 10012.

ISBN 978-0-545-14604-3

Text copyright © 2010 by Lara Bergen.
Illustrations copyright © 2010 by Scholastic Inc.
All rights reserved. Published by Scholastic Inc.
SCHOLASTIC and associated logos are trademarks
and/or registered trademarks of Scholastic Inc.

12 11 10 9 8 7 6 5   11 12 13 14 15/0

Printed in the U.S.A.   40
First printing, March 2010
Designed by Tim Hall

To Shannon the Awesome . . . editor!

CHAPTER 1

Sophie closed her book and sighed.

Leo the Lionhearted: Bravest Kid Ever.

It just wasn't fair!

Sophie was sick and tired of reading about other people who were so much more . . . more *everything* than her.

Then it hit her. She knew exactly what she needed.

A name.

Of course! But not just any old name. She had one of those already: Sophie H. Miller. (The *H* stood for Hamm—yes, Hamm. Enough said.)

Big deal. So what? Boring.

What Sophie needed was a name that described her perfectly. She needed a name that said it all. A name that was *not* boring.

She looked across the library table, took a deep breath, and sighed again.

"What?" said her friend Kate Barry. Her face popped up from behind her book. "Are you okay?"

But Sophie sighed a lot. So Kate wasn't too concerned.

"No. I am not okay," said Sophie. Now she crossed her arms.

"Why?" Kate looked around. "Is Toby bugging you again?" She scrunched her mouth into a small sour-lemon frown. Then she glared at the boy sitting at the next round table. Sophie's eyes followed hers.

Toby Myers was very freckled, very redheaded, and—if you asked Sophie—very hard to look at for very long. So she didn't.

Instead, she shook her head. "No. That's not it."

"Then why?" asked Kate. Beneath her long brown bangs, her forehead made a wavy wrinkle.

"Because I'm nothing," Sophie told her. This time, she gave an extra-long, I'll-never-be-anything sigh.

Kate looked at her funny.

"I'm talking about this," Sophie said. She picked up her book and jabbed her finger at the cover.

"You'd rather be a book?" Kate said. She scratched the freckle on her neck. "Can't help you there. Sorry."

"No," groaned Sophie. That wasn't it at all. She ran her finger along the book's title. "I want to be Sophie the . . . something, too! All the great characters have names like that. And I'm a character. Ms. Moffly says so all the time. Think about it!" Sophie grinned at her best friend. "Nate the Great. Ramona the Brave. Harriet the Spy . . ."

"Winnie the Pooh," added Kate. There was a twinkle in her eye.

"Exactly!" Sophie nodded. Then she frowned. "Very funny."

Kate giggled and Miss Elaine, the librarian, swooped over.

"*Shhh!*" warned Miss Elaine. "It's *quiet* reading time. Remember?"

Kate nodded and buried her nose back in her book. Sophie could tell she was still laughing.

"You're no help at all," Sophie whispered. But she had to giggle a little, too.

They watched the librarian zip off to Toby's table. "Please sit down," she told him and his super-annoying, new best friend, Archie Dolan. Someone was *always* telling the two of them to sit down.

Kate patted Sophie's hand. "Sorry," she whispered. "You know, I'm not anything, either. Though 'Kate the Great' is kind of catchy."

Sophie slumped down and opened her book again. But she didn't try to read it. She filled her cheeks with air and thought very hard instead.

Sophie the...

Sophie the...

Sophie the... *what*?!

She couldn't really be Sophie the First, because she was not the first in her family. Her older sister, Hayley, never let her forget that.

And she couldn't be Sophie the Last, because of Max, her little brother. Which was fine. She didn't really want to be last, anyway!

She couldn't even be the only Sophie in Ms. Moffly's third-grade class, thanks to Sophie Aarons. Or Sophie A., as everyone called her.

That was another reason Sophie needed a special name. Being called Sophie M. was just plain silly.

So what else was there?

Sophie couldn't be anything that rhymed with her name, like lucky duck Kate the Great. Nothing rhymed with "Sophie." At least, nothing that made sense.

She couldn't be the Tallest. That was Grace.

She couldn't be the Smartest. That was Sophie A., too. (So unfair!)

She couldn't even be the Meanest. (Not that she wanted to be.) That was Mindy.

And she couldn't be the Funniest. That was Kate. Definitely.

"Hey, I've got one," Kate suddenly whispered.

Sophie turned to her, still frowning. "What?"

"Sophie the *Grouch*," Kate answered.

Sophie rolled her eyes. Maybe Kate was not that funny after all. But Sophie knew that something would come to her sooner or later.

Meanwhile, Kate kept rambling on softly. "Ramona the Pest... Bob the Builder... Billy the Kid... Marvin the Magnificent... Glinda the Good Witch..."

"What did you say?" Sophie asked all of a sudden.

"Glinda the Good Witch?" Kate repeated. "You know, from *The Wizard of Oz*."

"No, no, no," said Sophie. She quickly looked over her shoulder. Was Miss Elaine staring at her? She turned back and carefully lowered her head and her voice. "What did you say before that?"

"Uh..." Kate thought for a moment. "Marvin the Magnificent?"

Sophie's heart began to *thump-a-thump-thump*. Of course! Why hadn't she thought of it before?

"So, what?" said Kate. "You want to be Marvin the Magnificent?"

"Of course not," said Sophie. Her name wasn't Marvin. And Magnificent was taken. But what about another word that meant the same thing—or even better? Something that wasn't boring or average at all.

Amazing.

Wonderful.

Marvelous.

Or maybe...Awesome.

That was it! That name was special. For sure!

Sophie felt her heart relax into a smooth and steady beat. She closed her book with a *whop* as Miss Elaine flashed the lights three times.

Library time was over.

But the time for Sophie the Awesome had just begun!

CHAPTER 2

Sophie walked back to her classroom feeling just as awesome as someone named Sophie the Awesome should. Plus she'd finally outsmarted snappy, snooty Mindy VonBoffmann. Talk about awesome!

Mindy was always doing something to torture her. And lately, her way of torturing Sophie had been to steal her library book right out from under her nose.

At the end of library period, each kid in the class always got to choose one book to check out.

The first time, Sophie had wanted *Amazing but True Dolphin Stories.* But Mindy got there first.

The second time, it had been *The Best Human Body Book Ever—with Deluxe See-through Pages.* But Mindy took it while Sophie was getting Toby's latest spitball out of her hair.

This time, it was almost *Awesome Animals You Can Draw.*

Almost.

But instead of reaching for the book she really wanted, Sophie knelt down and reached for a thick one called *Stamps, Stamps, and More Stamps.* And sure enough, Mindy's sneaky hand swept in to grab it.

"Oh—you didn't want this book, did you?" Mindy asked, acting surprised.

And for the first time, Sophie smiled at Mindy.

"No," she said pleasantly. "I didn't want it at all." Then she reached up and pulled down *Awesome Animals You Can Draw.*

And the point goes to me! Sophie thought as she headed for the door. She gave herself a bonus point when Miss Elaine said, "It is *so* nice that you're not fighting over books this week." *Whoo-hoo! Way to go!*

Back in the classroom, Sophie's day got even better. Usually, that was when Ms. Moffly made them write about something boring in their journals. Things like what they did over the weekend. Or what they liked best about third grade. Blah!

Sophie sometimes wished her teacher would let them write about a dream. Or about what they wished they'd done that weekend instead of going to their sister's super-boring ballet recital and cleaning their whole room. Or *anything* but third grade.

Sophie had tried to write about something else once. But somehow, Ms. Moffly had known it wasn't true.

"I like your imagination, Sophie," Ms. Moffly had written at the end of the page. *"I hope one day you do get to travel into space. But from now on, let's stick to the facts. Real life can be very interesting, too!"*

Oh, yeah?

There was just one word for Sophie's life: *boring*. There was nothing special or interesting about it at all.

Her height was average. Her weight was average. Even her hair was average. It wasn't straight. And it wasn't curly. It wasn't long. And it wasn't short. It wasn't blond. And it wasn't brown.

No matter how you sliced it, Sophie came out somewhere in the middle. Alphabetically by first name. Alphabetically by last name. By birthday. By shoe size. In every running race, or reading group, or spelling bee. Medium. Boring.

For a few years, Sophie had been the youngest in her family. But since her two-year-old brother, Max, had been born, she'd been in the middle there, too.

She even lived in a town called Ordinary, Virginia! Ugh.

But Sophie tried to erase all that from her mind as Ms. Moffly stood and addressed the room.

"I'm afraid that I didn't get to finish reading your journals this weekend," Ms. Moffly explained.

There was an "*Ooh!*" and a "*Ms. Moffly's in trouble!*" from Archie and Toby's corner of the room.

Sophie rolled her eyes.

"That's enough," the teacher said, smiling. "And, boys, please sit down. Now, as you all know, my sister got married and, well, there just wasn't enough time. So," Ms. Moffly went on, "I don't have the journals ready to give back to you. That means that for the next fifteen minutes, you are free to read your new library books, or start your math homework, or *quietly* play a board game."

The whole class cheered. Sophie, too. She knew exactly what she was going to do!

Kate pulled out her book, *101 Knock-Knock Jokes.* Grace and Sydney left their desks to play Mastermind on the floor. And Sophie got up to find a sheet of paper and the sharpest pencil in the pencil jar. Then she sat back down and practiced writing her new name.

Sophie the Awesome needed an awesome signature, after all!

Sophie the Awesome
Sophie the Awesome!
The Awesome Sophie!

Sophie studied the page. She always did like a good exclamation point!

Then she felt Kate tug on her shirtsleeve.

"Knock-knock," said Kate.

Sophie sighed. She was eager to get on to other Sophie the Awesome business. Like relabeling all her folders. But she guessed she had time for one joke.

"Who's there?" she asked.

"Cows go," said Kate.

"Cows go who?" said Sophie.

"No, cows go *moo*!" Kate doubled over, laughing.

"Good one," said Sophie, trying to sound official. "It has the approval of Sophie the Awesome."

Kate's eyes got wide. "Is that your 'the' name? Really?" she asked.

"Really!" said Sophie.

"Oh." Kate twisted her mouth to the side. Sophie knew that this meant she was thinking hard. "Are you sure?" Kate said after a minute.

"Sure I'm sure," said Sophie.

"But what's so awesome about you?" asked Kate.

Sophie stared at her. She was shocked! Appalled! "What do you mean?" she said. "I thought you were my best friend, Kate!"

"I *am*!" Kate told her. She laid her arm across Sophie's shoulders. "And you are for sure the most awesome best friend in the whole world. Except when you make me listen to you sing."

Kate giggled, but stopped when she saw that Sophie wasn't smiling.

"You could definitely call yourself Sophie the Awesome *Friend*, if you wanted," Kate added quickly.

Sophie thought about it for a second. "No." She shook her head. "I think just 'Sophie the Awesome' is better."

But Kate looked doubtful. "I don't know." She shrugged. "It's just, when you say that someone is plain awesome, you expect them to really be awesome...in every way."

Sophie shrugged. "Maybe I *am* awesome in every way," she said. She turned to the back of the room and pointed to Toby and Archie. They were bombing chessmen with dice and colored dominos. "I know I am, compared to them!"

Then Sophie reached for her library book. "And how about *this*?" she said. "I can draw awesome animals. Check it out!"

She opened the book to a page about horses and drew carefully, step by step. Then she showed Kate the awesome finished product.

"Ta-da! A horse!" she said.

Kate frowned. "It looks more like a cat."

"Yeah, you're right," Sophie said. She had to agree. "I guess I better practice."

"All I'm saying," Kate went on, "is that if you want people to call you awesome — especially people like them — you're going to have to prove it." She pointed her thumbs in two directions. One toward Toby and Archie, and the other toward Mindy and Lily Lemley, Mindy's copycat friend.

Sophie looked in one direction, then the other. Kate was right. Sophie could totally see Toby and Archie making fun of her new name, unless she had proof of her awesomeness to back it up.

As for Mindy, anyone sneaky enough to steal a library book was sneaky enough to try to steal an awesome name, too. Sophie had to make her name her own. It was true.

Sophie looked back down at her writing. She guessed it would take more than words on paper to get "Sophie the Awesome" to stick.

Just then, Ms. Moffly clapped her hands. "Time for music," she called.

Sophie stood up, took a deep breath, and looked hard into Kate's eyes. "Okay," she said solemnly. "If I need to prove I'm awesome, then that's exactly what I'll do!"

CHAPTER 3

As third graders, Sophie's class got to walk through the halls alone. This was a "privilege," Ms. Moffly told them. It made Sophie feel very grown up, and a little less boring. But only a little.

Sophie especially liked being Line Leader. Too bad it was Jack's turn that week. She really could have been awesome at leading the line. Plus Jack could be so slow. And Sophie could not wait to get to music and be awesome at that. It was all she could do not to say, "Hurry up! Hurry up!"

Sophie knew that it would not be easy to be awesome at music, mostly because of one thing. A thing called "mouthing the words."

Sophie used to try to sing out loud. She would close her eyes and open her mouth and hope the right sounds would come out. The thing was, they never did. Instead, the strangest sounds came out. Sounds that made people turn and stare. Sounds that didn't always sound so good.

But today Sophie would sing. And it would be awesome!

Then she walked into the music room and her face instantly lit up. Maybe she would not have to sing, after all!

Sophie looked around at the instruments scattered on the floor. How could she have forgotten? It was Monday, and Monday was Rhythm Day. *Awesome!* Sophie thought.

"Good morning, Ms. Moffly's class," said Mrs. Wittels, their music teacher. She had on a blouse with a very big, very pink, very floppy bow. It was exactly the same color as the makeup on her cheeks. It looked strange. But also fancy. Which was how Mrs. Wittels always looked.

"Good morning," replied a few students. Most were already busy diving for the instruments on the floor.

"Please don't touch the instruments until I tell you to!" Mrs. Wittels called.

"Awww!" groaned the class.

On Rhythm Day, no one had to sit at a desk. They all got to sit in a big circle on the floor. They didn't have to tell Mrs. Wittels if a note was an A or a B or a Z. A quarter, a half, or a double. Instead, they each got to make up rhythms for the rest of the class to follow. And they got to play all kinds of awesome instruments—bells and maracas and triangles and cymbals and sand blocks and tambourines and tom-toms and castanets and claves.

And best of all, they didn't have to sing!

Sophie scooted down in front of the biggest, most awesome tambourine in the room. This was just what she needed!

"Are you ready to make some *rrrhythms*?" trilled Mrs. Wittels.

"Yeah!" the whole class cheered.

"Then let's get started," the teacher said. "Who would like to be first?"

Sophie's hand was already up and waving. "Ooh!" she called. She couldn't help it. "Ooh! Mrs. Wittels, pick me!"

Of course Mrs. Wittels didn't. Mrs. Wittels liked kids to make *musical* noise, but she did not like them to talk much.

"Mindy," she said, casting a quick look at Sophie. "Thank you for *quietly* raising your hand. Please give us a rhythm to follow."

Mindy sat up straight and smiled. Sophie just rolled her eyes. Then Mindy held up a bright, shiny triangle and tapped out a gentle *ting, ting, ting-a-ling-a-ting-ting*.

"Very nice," said Mrs. Wittels, nodding. She raised her arms like a conductor. This was her signal for the rest of the class to follow. She closed her eyes. "And-a-one, and-a-two, and-a—"

CLANG, CLANG, CLANG-A-CLANG CLANG!!!!! went Sophie on her tambourine, feeling especially awesome.

Mrs. Wittels' eyes flew open. "What was *that*? Archie? Toby?" She turned to the usual suspects in the class and frowned.

"It wasn't me," said Toby, pointing to his drum.

"That was Sophie M.," piped up Mindy matter-of-factly. "And it wasn't even right."

Grrr! Sophie wanted to growl at her very much.

"Sophie," said Mrs. Wittels. She shook her head. "Please don't play so hard. You could break the tambourine."

Hmm. Sophie doubted that. She had seen Archie do much worse. Her hand was another story, though. *Ouch!* She shook it out and hoped it wasn't broken.

"Let's switch instruments now, shall we?" Mrs. Wittels suggested. "And, Mindy, why don't you choose who leads the rhythm next."

The kids set down their instruments, and a few raised their hands, hoping Mindy would pick them.

But Sophie didn't bother. Instead, she scanned the floor for a new instrument. Something awesome, but with a little less pain and more gain. Besides, she already knew who Mindy would pick.

"Lily," said Mindy.

Of course.

Lily Lemley looked nothing like Mindy VonBoffmann. But she tried as hard as she could.

She wore a headband, just like Mindy. Every single day. Unless Mindy didn't wear a headband. Then Lily took hers off.

She wore mismatched socks, just like Mindy. Even though Sophie and Kate had totally thought of doing it first.

She had the same shoes as Mindy. And the same backpack. And the same TV show lunch box. And the same "I love Disney World" sweatshirt. Even though Sophie knew for a fact that Lily had never gone there. Not once.

Lily held up the triangle she'd picked and tapped it. *Ting, ting, ting-a-ling-a-ting-ting.*

It was Mindy's rhythm all over again. Exactly.

Mrs. Wittels shook her head. "Lily, remember when I told you last week to make up your own rhythm?"

"Um, okay," Lily said.

Everybody waited. And waited a little more.

"Just do *something*!" Mrs. Wittels said.

Lily held up her triangle. *Ting, ting . . . ting, ting-a-ling-a-ting-ting,* she went at last.

"Wonderful," sighed Mrs. Wittels. "And-a-one, and-a-two, and-a—"

CLACK, CLACK . . . CLACK, CLACK-A-CLACK-A-CLACK-CLACK! went Sophie, banging her claves as awesomely as she could.

She looked around proudly. She'd gotten *that* right, she was sure. But no one seemed impressed. Sophie sighed. How could she really prove her awesomeness by copying someone else's rhythm, anyway?

She'd just have to wait for her own turn to lead. And, of course, her turn came when it usually did. Not at the beginning. And not at the end. But somewhere in the middle.

"Sophie M.," Kate said as soon as her turn was over.

Sophie grinned, and her heart beat faster. She was suddenly a little nervous. But there was no looking back now. Her time to be awesome had come! She dove for the new instrument she'd had her eyes on.

"Are you sure about those?" asked Mrs. Wittels.

Sophie waved her cymbals and nodded. Of course she was sure. Let the world's most awesome rhythm begin!

CRASH-CRASH-CRASH, CRASH-A-CRASH, CRASH-A-CRASH, CRASH-A-CRASH-CRASH-CRASH-CRASH, CRASH, CRASH, CRASH, CRASH-A-CRASH-A-CRASH, CRASH-A-CRASH, CRASH, CRASH, CRASH, CRASH, CRASH, CRASH-A-CRASH-A-CRASH-A-CRASH-A—

"Sophie!" cried Mrs. Wittels.

Sophie stopped, mid-*CRASH*, smiling widely.

Mrs. Wittels had noticed her awesomeness! And she wasn't even done yet.

Sophie made one final *CRASH!* Then she peered around at her classmates. She guessed they were too amazed by her awesomeness to clap. Then she noticed that their hands were over their ears. Even Kate's.

"Sophie!" Mrs. Wittels repeated. "Please put down the cymbals! That is quite enough!"

Sophie looked up at the teacher. Her face was very white except for the pink circles on her cheeks. Her whole body was shaking. So was her pink bow.

Slowly, Sophie did as she was told. She wondered if Mrs. Wittels was just stunned by her awesome performance. But something in Sophie's stomach told her no.

Toby lunged for the cymbals. "Do we get to copy her rhythm now?" he asked.

"No!" snapped Mrs. Wittels. She snatched the cymbals away. "I think we've had enough rhythm for one day." She rubbed her forehead. "We have ten more minutes, class. Let's just sit quietly until then, shall we?"

"But I didn't get a turn!" Jack complained.

"Me neither!" said Grace.

Mrs. Wittels held up her hand. "We'll start with you next week."

"Thanks a lot, Sophie," groaned Dean.

Sophie sighed and looked at the floor. So maybe she wasn't awesome . . . at music.

But that was okay. She had ten whole minutes to figure something else out!

CHAPTER 4

"Look out!" hollered Sophie. "Coming through!"

At last, music was over. The final ten minutes had felt like a year. But now Sophie's class was on their way back to their classroom. And Sophie was on her way to awesomeness. She was sure of it.

She grabbed the stairway banister and swung herself down to the landing.

"Ouch!" someone yelped.

"Oh, sorry," said Sophie.

She hadn't meant to land on Sophie A.'s foot. But had Sophie A. seen how far she'd jumped?

"Did you see how far I jumped?" Sophie asked her.

"*No,*" Sophie A. said.

"I did, and that was nothing," said Toby, trotting down the stairs behind them. He grabbed the same banister and leaped over the landing. "Check *that* out!" he said.

Then he ran back up the stairs and did it again.

Sophie gave him an I'll-show-you face and ran back up, as well.

"Hey, guys, you better stop that!" Grace said. She was the class Caboose that week. That meant she walked at the end of the line wherever the class went. "You know you're not supposed to goof around on the stairs."

"Yeah," added Mindy, who was not the Caboose. Sophie thought that meant she should really keep her mouth shut. But she never did. "Cut it out, or I'm telling Ms. Moffly when we get back to the room," Mindy said.

"Me too," said Lily.

"You'll make us lose our hall privilege," Mindy went on.

"Yeah, you will," said Lily.

But Sophie wasn't goofing around at all. She was trying to prove a point: that she was awesome... at jumping down the stairs.

"Hey, everybody!" she called out. "Look at this!"

"Mindy and Lily really will tell on you," Kate warned her in a low voice. "You know they will."

But Sophie didn't care. She backed up to the second, then the third, then the fourth step. She waited for a minute, until almost every eye was on her. Then she jumped.

"Ta-da!"

Toby followed her.

"Ta-da shma-da. Anyone can do that," he said.

Oh, yeah? thought Sophie. She ran back up to the fifth step. But Toby was already there.

"Ay, caramba!" he hollered, leaping. He landed and grinned. "Five steps. New school record. Beat that, Sophster," he said.

"Guys!" Grace groaned. "Let's go now!"

But Sophie wasn't ready to go. She ran up to the sixth step.

"What are you doing?" Kate asked.

Sophie held out her arms. "Behold! I am about to perform the most awesome step jump ever."

"Are you crazy?" said Kate. "You can't jump six steps. You're going to break your neck!"

"You're going to be in big trouble!" said Mindy.

But Sophie just grinned. "I can do it!" she said.

Then she made the big mistake of looking down. What was she thinking? Six steps was way too much!

But Sophie could never, ever say she was awesome if she gave up now.

She closed her eyes and...wait! What was she thinking? She had to look!

So she opened her eyes and jumped.

The good news was that Sophie landed on her feet. The bad news was that she also landed on her bottom. *Ouch!* Dumb, slippery new shoes. Boy, that hurt. A lot.

Sophie did not want to cry. But it was hard not to when she looked up at Kate.

Kate knelt down beside her. "Would you like to go to the nurse?" she asked softly.

Sophie sniffed and nodded. "Yeah, maybe," she said. And not just because her bottom hurt. It would also get her away from everyone. Including Archie and Toby.

"Ha-ha!" Toby laughed and gave Archie a high five. "Crash landings don't count. I still have the record!"

Sophie made a face at him. Good old Kate stuck out her tongue. Then she helped Sophie up.

"Out of our way," Kate said. "Could someone tell Ms. Moffly I took Sophie to the nurse?"

"Oh, we'll tell her, all right," said Mindy, grinning smugly.

Kate held Sophie's hand and led her back up the stairs toward the nurse's office.

"Hey. Knock-knock," she said after a second.

"Who's there?" Sophie sighed.

"Orange," said Kate.

"Orange who?" Sophie asked.

"Orange you glad you didn't break your neck?"

Sophie sighed. Yes, she was glad she had not broken her neck. And she was glad that she did not have to go back to her classroom yet — and see Ms. Moffly.

Plus she needed time to think of something else awesome to do.

Kate left her at the nurse's office. Mrs. Frost, the nurse, crossed her arms in front of her. She had a very big front to cross. But somehow it worked.

"Well, if it isn't Sophie Miller. What happened to you?" asked the nurse.

"I, um, fell on the stairs," Sophie said.

Mrs. Frost clucked her tongue. "I hope you weren't jumping," she said.

Sophie filled her cheeks with air.

"Tell me, where does it hurt?" asked the nurse.

Sophie pointed to her backside, and the nurse took a look. She made Sophie bend and squat and twist.

"Looks like you'll be fine," said Mrs. Frost. "Do you want me to call your parents?"

Sophie thought for a minute. Then she shook her head. She was already feeling better. And she really didn't want her day to end like this. She'd had a rocky start at being awesome. But she wasn't giving up yet!

"Could I maybe just lie down for a little while?" Sophie said. That would give her time to think. And time for her face to get less red.

The nurse had Sophie lie facedown on the cot in the corner. It was lumpy, but cool and clean. Sophie tried not to think about all the throw-up it must have seen. (Like hers. Last year. The day after Halloween.)

Suddenly, Sophie felt a chill on her bottom. She jumped.

"Ice pack," explained the nurse. "Now be still. Do you need another?"

"No, thanks," Sophie answered. One was plenty cold enough.

She lay there for a few minutes and tried to think

of more ways to be awesome. But it was kind of hard with a freezing-cold ice pack on her bottom.

Sophie looked up at the big white clock on the wall. Twelve o'clock. Her stomach rumbled.

"Uh, Mrs. Frost?" she said.

"Yes?" answered the nurse. "Did you change your mind about that second ice pack?"

"Um, no," Sophie said. "I was just thinking that I feel better. Can I go to lunch now?"

"Very well," said the nurse. She took back the ice pack and helped Sophie to her feet. "So, what lesson did you learn today, Sophie?" she asked.

Sophie rubbed the back of her pants. "I guess I learned my bottom is not that tough," she said.

CHAPTER 5

Sophie was still a tiny bit sore when she got to the lunchroom. But the smell of hot food helped a lot. Kate did, too.

"Hey, Sophie!" Kate called. She waved her over to the lunch line. "Sophie! Over here!"

"*Excuse* me!" said Mindy. She was standing just behind Kate. "No cuts!"

"Yeah," said Lily, who was behind Mindy. "No cuts."

Kate turned to them. "I was *saving* this place. So it's *not* cuts." She took Sophie's arm and pulled her in. "Besides, give her a break. How are you feeling, Sophie?" she asked.

Sophie stretched out a smile. "Awesome," she said.

"Whatever," Mindy scoffed. "We'll give you a break, Sophie. 'Cause we know Ms. Moffly's not going to." Then she giggled, and Lily chimed in.

Sophie turned to Kate. She suddenly wasn't feeling as awesome anymore. "Am I in really big trouble?" she whispered.

Kate bit her lip and shrugged. "Actually, we all are," she whispered back. "Ms. Moffly says no hall privileges for the whole class for the rest of the week."

Sophie sighed. That was too bad, and not just because she liked hall privileges. It was too bad because it made being awesome even harder.

Kate kindly handed Sophie a tray. "Hey, knock-knock!" she said brightly.

"Who's there?" Sophie said.

"Kenya," Kate said.

"Kenya who?" said Sophie.

"Kenya hand me one of those milks, please?" Kate laughed.

Sophie smiled a little again. She was glad she had a friend like Kate to cheer her up.

"Keep it moving!" shouted Grace from the back of the line.

Sophie handed Kate a carton of milk and slid her tray to where the lunch lady stood, waiting. She offered Sophie a plate full of fish sticks and French fries.

Sophie's smile quickly faded. Fish sticks? How could something so blah have smelled so yum? It was probably the most unawesome lunch she could think of.

She set the plate down on her tray, then took a roll and a dish of carrots.

Then, suddenly, an idea hit her—and it was awesome!

"Hey, give me your tray!" she told Kate. Sophie grabbed it before Kate could stop her. "Sydney, give me yours, too!"

"Huh?" said Sydney. She was just about to walk out to the tables.

"I mean, won't you *please* let me carry your tray out for you?" said Sophie. She smiled a big and helpful-looking smile. "You too, Sophie A."

"Why?" the girls asked together.

"Because," said Sophie, "I just want to be helpful. Plus, carrying four trays would be pretty awesome, don't you think?"

She grinned at Kate. If she could have winked, she would have. It was too bad that it looked like something was stuck in her eye whenever she tried.

"Are you sure you can do it?" asked Sydney.

"No problem!" said Sophie. She moved Kate's tray to her left arm and balanced it just above her elbow. Then she took Sydney's tray in her left hand and Sophie A.'s in her right.

Ugh. She tried not to groan. The trays were much heavier than she'd expected.

"Uh . . . put my tray right here, will you?" she asked Kate.

"Like this?" said Kate. She balanced the tray in the crook of Sophie's right arm.

"Perfect," said Sophie.

"Are you sure you can do this?" Sydney asked one more time.

I hope, Sophie thought. "I am sure," she said.

In fact, maybe she could carry *five* trays. One on her head! Like that lady carrying water in the desert on TV.

But then she looked around. The nearest tray was Mindy's.

Four trays would be awesome enough.

"Okay! Let's go!" Sophie said.

Sophie led her short line of trayless friends toward the girls' usual table. Her arms were starting to shake. But she held her head high.

She waited for the whole cafeteria to notice her. To stop midchew and stare. To yell, "That is awesome!"

But no one did.

Sophie guessed they needed prodding.

"Coming through!" she began to holler. "Hot

fish sticks! Look out!" Suddenly, Dean scooted his chair out in front of her. "Seriously, look out!" she cried.

Dean scooted his chair back in. "No, *you* look out," he said.

"What are you doing?" asked Jack, who was sitting beside him.

Sophie reached her table at last and smiled. "I," she said, "am carrying four — count them — four trays!"

She wanted to bow, but of course she couldn't. So Sophie decided to set the trays down. But she couldn't do that, either.

The minute she leaned forward, the plates started sliding. The silverware started rolling. And all four trays started moving on their own!

"Help me, Kate!" Sophie cried.

Kate quickly slipped her hand under Sydney's tray and set it down. Sophie A. and Sydney hurried to grab the others — just in time!

Sophie waited for her heart to start beating

normally again. Then she held up her arms. "Ta-da!" she called. She looked at all the kids around her. "What do you think? Wasn't that...awesome?"

She thought there would be cheering or clapping. But there was not.

"You almost dropped them all," said Sophie A.

"You spilled my carrots," said Sydney.

"What's so awesome about carrying four trays, anyway?" asked Mindy. She had just walked up behind them, carrying her own tray. "You know, I went to a restaurant last night where the waiter carried all five plates out at one time. It was for my grandmother's birthday and it was very fancy." Mindy turned and flashed Sophie one of her squinty, no-teeth smiles. "*And* he set the dessert on fire!"

"Really?" said Kate. "On real fire?"

Sophie nudged Kate with her elbow.

"Sorry," said Kate, shrugging. "But that does sound pretty awesome."

"I'll tell you what else is awesome," Toby piped

up suddenly. He was sitting at the boys' table and holding up a handful of fries. "Look at this!"

He opened his mouth as wide as it could go. (*Yuck!* thought Sophie.) Then, one by one, he began to shove in French fries.

"One . . . two . . . three . . . ," Archie counted.

Soon the whole boys' table had joined in, soft enough so that no lunch monitor would hear.

". . . twenty-one . . . twenty-two . . . twenty-three!"

Toby pumped his arms. That was about all he could do with a big mouthful of fries.

"Twenty-three!" cheered Archie.

"That's a record!" said Jack.

"That is gross," said Mindy.

"No, that's awesome!" said Dean.

Toby, of course, said nothing. He looked happy. But uncomfortable, too. He couldn't even chew.

Awesome? Toby? Sophie didn't think so!

She sat down and grabbed her own fries. And Kate's. And she began to stuff them into her mouth.

"Count," she mumbled to Kate.

"Uh, one...two...three..." Kate began.

Soon all the girls were joining in.

"...eleven...twelve...thirteen..."

Then the boys were counting, too.

"...eighteen...nineteen...twenty..."

Sophie took another fry and put it into her mouth. She really wanted to chew. But she was so close—she couldn't stop now! If this was what it took to be awesome, then this was what she would do.

"...twenty-one...twenty-two..." The voices were getting louder.

Sophie picked up another French fry. So what if her jaw was burning? She was going to break Toby's record.

She was going to be awesome!

She wanted to smile. But she couldn't. So she wiggled French fry number twenty-three instead.

"Hey! That one doesn't count!" shouted Toby. By then, he had emptied his own mouth. "It's too small!"

"Way too small!" agreed Archie.

Sophie wanted to frown. But she couldn't. So she glared at Toby and Archie instead.

Then she quickly picked up another fry and began to shove it into her mouth.

"...twenty-thr—"

Suddenly, the voices around her stopped. It was like someone had hit the "mute" button, or—Or!

There was something else that could make the lunchroom get quiet.

Sophie slowly turned.

Sure enough, it was Principal Tate.

Uh-oh...

CHAPTER 6

"Miss Miller," said the principal. He was looking down his long nose at Sophie. His eyes were very serious. "Do I need to remind you of the importance of table manners?"

Sophie looked up at him with a wide, stuffed mouth and even wider eyes. She had never, ever had the principal speak to her before. But she had seen him speak to other kids (like Toby and Archie) a lot. So she knew that when he asked you a question, you'd better answer.

But how was she going to answer him with twenty-three French fries in her mouth?

She figured the best thing to do was just shake her head.

"I didn't think so," said Principal Tate. "And I hope that I also don't need to remind you of the *consequences* of poor manners."

Consequences! That was not one of Sophie's favorite words.

"Such as sitting out recess?" the principal went on. He raised one eyebrow, then the other.

How did he do that? And how was Sophie going to get rid of her French fries, she wondered. Chew? No. Spit? She wished.

She shook her head again and felt warm drool run down her chin.

"I know you wouldn't like that," said the principal. "And neither would I. That's why I suggest you carefully remove those extra French fries from your mouth. And from now on, please eat them as they should be eaten: one at a time."

This time Sophie nodded. And Principal Tate nodded back.

"Very good, Miss Miller," he said. "Enjoy your lunch."

☆ ☆ ☆

Sophie did not enjoy her lunch, of course. She did not enjoy everyone snickering at her. And she did not enjoy staring at her pile of spit-covered fries.

She was glad when lunch was over and it was time for recess. But still, she wasn't awesome yet. And it was hard to be *very* glad without that.

"Come on," said Kate as they hurried outside. "Let's play our game."

For two weeks, they had been playing the same recess game every day: International Superspy and Wild-Animal Emergency Vet.

Sophie always looked forward to it. Kate was the vet, specializing in big cats and dolphins. And Sophie was the spy, on a tough, top secret case.

But not today, she decided.

"I can't play. I need to think," she told Kate.

"Think? About what?" asked Kate.

Sophie looked at her. "About how to be awesome!"

"Oh, right," said Kate. She twisted her mouth to the side and looked thoughtful. "Hey! How about Sophie the Big Mouth? Get it?" She laughed. "French fries. Big mouth."

"Very funny." Sophie sighed. "But I could have set a new French fry record," she added. "Besides, Sophie the Awesome is the perfect name for me. I know it! I just have to find the right thing to be awesome at. Something that won't get me in any more trouble."

She looked around the yard as she talked. At the basketball court. And the jump-rope corner. And the jungle gym.

"That's it!" Sophie said. The jungle gym! There were a million ways to be awesome there! She took off, with Kate right behind her.

The school's jungle gym was brand new that year. It had a straight slide and a twisty one. It had a rope and a rock wall and a regular ladder to climb up. It had a corkscrew thing to twirl down, and a real fire pole. Plus monkey bars to swing across. And not one, but two forts on stilts on either side.

The jungle gym was something Sophie was very good at. And it was something she could be awesome at if she tried!

She jumped up and grabbed the monkey bars. After a few tries, she swung herself up and happily looked down from the top. Awesome!

"Hey, over here!" she called to the rest of the playground. "Look how high I am! Isn't it awesome? Check it out!"

But nobody heard her. The basketball players were too busy. And the jump-ropers were too loud.

"Check what out?"

Sophie turned to see Kate right beside her.

"How did you get up here?" Sophie asked.

"I followed you," said Kate.

Sophie sighed. "You're not supposed to follow me. I'm trying to be awesome," she said.

"Oh," said Kate. Then she looked around. "You might have to try a little harder. This is pretty easy."

"Oh," Sophie said. She was pretty sure that Kate was right.

She looked around the jungle gym. "What if I climb to the top of the fort?"

That was not easy. In fact, it was so hard no one had ever done it before. Sophie would be the first. And it would be awesome!

"Mmm, I don't know," said Kate.

Just then, a voice called up to them from below.

"Hey, Kate! Hey, Sophie!" It was Ben. "Want to play tag with us?"

Ben was Sophie's favorite boy in their class, by far. Mostly because he was nice to girls. But also because he wore cool glasses and had a real air hockey table at his house. Plus he did not hang out that much with Toby. That was the best thing of all about Ben.

He was playing tag with Eve and Mia.

"The slide is safety," Ben called up.

"I'm not It!" Kate hollered. She turned to Sophie. "Come on, let's go!"

"Not now," said Sophie.

"Why not?" asked Kate.

"Because I have a plan!" Sophie pointed to the fort roof. "I can't waste time playing tag. No one can be awesome at that," Sophie said matter-of-factly.

"You never know," said Kate. She looked up at the roof, too. "Besides, don't you think that looks kind of scary? What if you fell again?"

Sophie chewed on her fingernail. Kate could be right. But what about being awesome? And why couldn't those jump-ropers be quiet? They really made it hard to think. And she was so tired of that song!

Bubble gum, bubble gum, in a dish,
How many pieces do you wish?

It rang out all the way across the yard. Mindy, Lily, Sophie A., Sydney, and Grace were jumping and chanting to the beat. Sophie liked to jump rope sometimes. But they did it *every* day.

Sophie glared at them, just out of habit. Then her glare turned into a grin.

That was it!

She gave Kate a hug and climbed down from the jungle gym. "You go play tag," she said. "*I'm* going to jump rope instead!"

Sydney was jumping when Sophie walked up to the group.

"Forty-one . . . forty-two . . . forty—Aw, too bad," said Lily, Sophie A., and Grace as Sydney tripped on the rope.

"My turn!" said Mindy.

"Hi, guys," said Sophie. "Can I jump, too?"

"Sure," said Sydney. She moved aside to make room for Sophie.

"Hang on!" said Mindy. "I said it's *my* turn."

"But you already went once," said Sydney. "Sophie M. just got here. Let her go."

Mindy's pinchy lips got pinchier. "Oh, fine." She turned to Sophie and shrugged. "Your turns never take long, anyway."

Normally, this would have bothered Sophie.

But this time, she smiled. She knew something that Mindy didn't. She was about to break Mindy's all-time jump-rope record!

"Hey, Mindy," Sophie said as she took her position. "What's your jump-rope record again?"

Mindy, who was now holding the rope, got a gleam in her eye.

"One hundred and thirty-four!" said Lily, who was holding the rope's other end.

"Exactly," Mindy said.

Of course, everybody knew that. Mindy reminded them all the time. She had set the record the year before. And no one in their class had ever beaten it. Not yet. But if Sophie could, she would officially be awesome. Even Mindy would have to admit it.

Sophie took a deep breath. She thought about the times she and Kate had jumped rope at home. There, they each used their own rope. They jumped and jumped for hours. Sophie was sure she'd jumped way more than one hundred and thirty-four times in a row before.

"Okay. Ready," she said.

Mindy and Lily turned the rope, and Sophie began to jump.

Bubble gum, bubble gum, in a dish,
How many pieces do you wish?

Sophie tried to focus. Sometimes she didn't even make it this far. But this day, her legs felt like springs. *You can do this!* Sophie told them.

The girls around her began to count. The numbers got bigger and bigger.

Twenty-one... twenty-two... twenty-three...

But Sophie was just getting started.

☆　☆　☆

Eighty-one... eighty-two... eighty-three...

"Wow, Sophie!" said Sydney. "Look at you go. Hey, everyone! Look at Sophie! She's almost at a hundred!"

"Yeah, Sophie A.!" cried a few girls as they ran over.

Sophie almost stopped jumping to correct them. Then they saw who she really was.

"Hey, look! It's Sophie M.!" they called.

Sophie couldn't help smiling as more kids began to gather. Soon everyone was cheering, "Go, Sophie M.! Go!"

And she did. Sophie jumped and jumped like she'd never jumped before.

She passed a hundred!

She was going to set the all-time record!

One hundred and thirty . . . one hundred and thirty-one . . . one hundred and —

Then the rope caught her leg.

"My turn!" Mindy sang out right away.

Sophie turned and glared at Mindy. This time, it was not out of habit.

"You tripped me!" she cried.

"I did not!" Mindy said. And then . . . did she smile at Lily? Sophie was sure that she did. That proved it — Mindy had tripped her on purpose!

"I want to go again!" Sophie told her.

"All right, class! Recess is over! Time to come in!" Ms. Moffly's voice rang out across the playground.

"You heard Ms. Moffly. You don't want to get in even more trouble," Mindy said too sweetly.

"But . . . ," Sophie began.

But nothing. It was too late. Mindy and most of the other kids were already running in.

Kate put her arm around Sophie's shoulder. "Don't worry," she said. "You can break the record tomorrow. Look how close you came!"

Yes, she was close. But that wasn't enough for Sophie.

Close wasn't the same as awesome. Not at all.

CHAPTER 7

Sophie was the last one to reach room 10 after recess. Partly because her legs felt like floppy fish sticks, and partly because room 10 was the last place she wanted to be.

Sophie would much rather be outside, jumping rope and being awesome. She definitely did not want to be inside, listening to Ms. Moffly tell her how much trouble she was in.

At times like this, Sophie wished she were back in second grade. She missed her teacher, Mrs. Cruz, a lot. It wasn't that Ms. Moffly was mean. Not exactly. But she sure had a lot of third-grade rules.

"There you are, Sophie," said Ms. Moffly. She was waiting for Sophie just outside the classroom door. "I believe we have something to talk about, don't we?"

Sophie sighed. "Yes, Ms. Moffly." She looked at her teacher's shoes. They had little heels and were blue and shiny.

"You were jumping in the stairwell?" Ms. Moffly asked.

"Yes," Sophie said. She thought about how nice it would be to have shoes just like Ms. Moffly's.

"And I hope you understand now why that is against the rules," Ms. Moffly went on.

"Yes," Sophie said. She'd also like those shoes in green, she decided. And maybe red.

"I hope that when you earn back your hallway privilege next week, this won't happen again," said Ms. Moffly.

"Yes," Sophie said. "I mean, no. I mean—What was the question?"

Oops.

Ms. Moffly knelt down until they were exactly

nose to nose and smiled. "I'm just glad that you're okay. No more jumping," she said.

Sophie nodded and smiled back. Inside, she sighed a relieved sigh.

"Now then," Ms. Moffly went on. "It's time to get to work." She led Sophie into the classroom. "Okay, class. Settle down and get out your notebooks. Archie and Toby, please sit down. We're interviewing this afternoon, remember?"

Oh, right! Sophie had forgotten. Sydney's mom had come in the week before and talked about her job. She was a reporter for the newspaper and she interviewed people a lot. That meant that she asked lots of questions. To Sophie, that sounded like a really fun job.

The best part, Sydney's mom said, was when a reporter got a "scoop." That meant they got an answer that no one else had ever gotten.

Sophie had asked if it meant they got a scoop of ice cream, too.

"Unfortunately, no," Sydney's mom had said, laughing a little.

Still, Sophie liked the sound of a reporter's job. And so did Ms. Moffly. So much, in fact, that she thought the class should give it a try. They had come up with questions on Friday. And now they were going to try them out on their classmates.

And what better day for Sophie to be interviewed than the one when she became Sophie the Awesome? Or almost awesome, anyway.

She grabbed her notebook, jotted down an extra question, and ran over to Kate. Of course they would interview each other. She could give Kate a really huge, really awesome scoop!

Then Ms. Moffly spoke again.

"Not so fast, everyone," she said. "I've chosen interview partners for you. Grace, you'll be with Ben. Sophie A., you'll be with Kate. Sophie M., you'll be with Toby..."

Sophie didn't hear a word she said after that.

Toby? Toby! No! she screamed inside her head. She couldn't even *look* at Toby. How could she interview him?

She glanced toward Toby's desk. He was pretending to throw up in his hands.

No. This was not going to work—at all. Sophie squared her shoulders and walked up to Ms. Moffly's desk.

"Er...Ms. Moffly," she said. "I need another partner."

"Excuse me?" said Ms. Moffly.

"You put me with Toby," Sophie explained. "And I can't interview him."

"You can't?" asked Ms. Moffly. "Why not?"

Why not? thought Sophie. She didn't know where to begin!

"Because we don't talk," Sophie said simply.

"Ah, yes, I've noticed," said Ms. Moffly. "But that's perfect, don't you think? You'll get to know each other better."

Better? Sophie shook her head. "Oh, I know all about him already," she said.

And she did. She knew that he was a big, giant pain in the neck.

"I see," said Ms. Moffly. "But I'll bet there are some things you still don't know. . . ."

"No, there aren't," said Sophie quickly. "I've known him since preschool." She glanced at Toby again, then turned back to Ms. Moffly and said very softly, "We used to be best friends."

Sophie didn't say it, but something had happened the year before. Toby had stopped talking to her—and started laughing at her instead. Now he acted like he hated her. And Sophie didn't act back. She just plain hated him.

Still, Sophie knew every single boring thing there was to know about Toby. She knew that his favorite color was red. She knew that he loved pistachio ice cream and that he hated anything chocolate. She knew that the scar on his cheek came from tripping in the sandbox. And she even knew his big family secret: His cousin, Dylan, had eleven toes!

But most of all, she knew that he was a big, giant pain in the neck.

"There is nothing," Sophie told Ms. Moffly, "that I don't know about Toby."

"I see," said Ms. Moffly. She put one finger on the side of her chin, and Sophie admired her pink nail polish. "Well, let's see how good a reporter you can be, then, Sophie. Try to find out something you didn't know before!"

She smiled down at Sophie. It was the same smile Sophie's mom had whenever she gave her a new chore.

Sophie turned and sulked off slowly.

She couldn't believe it. How could she be awesome now, when she was paired with the worst partner in the class?

CHAPTER 8

S ophie slumped down in the desk next to Toby. She looked at the questions in her notebook, but she didn't say a word.

"Go ahead already," Toby groaned.

"Okay, okay," said Sophie. She knew all the answers already. But since Ms. Moffly was watching, she had to play along.

"Favorite color?" she asked Toby, trying not to look at him.

"Red," Toby said.

Sophie sighed a bored sigh. *Of course,* she thought.

"Favorite ice cream?"

"Chocolate."

"What?" Sophie must have heard him wrong.

"Chocolate," Toby repeated.

"I thought you hated chocolate," said Sophie.

Toby shrugged. "Not anymore."

Sophie frowned as she wrote down *chocklit*. Something about it didn't look right. But she left it and moved on.

"Do you have any pets?" Sophie asked. She pictured Toby's two cats and his dog, Barnaby, in her head.

"Two cats," he said.

"And one dog," Sophie added. She rolled her eyes.

But Toby shook his head. "No. Just two cats," he said. He looked at his lap and took a deep breath. "Barnaby...died this summer."

"Really?" Sophie said. Oh. "I'm so sorry...."

Good old shaggy, smelly Barnaby. Dead? She hadn't known.

"He was old," said Toby softly. Then he frowned. "Are you done?"

"Uh, not quite," Sophie told him. She tried to read her next question, but it was hard. She was still so stunned.

"Um..." she said at last. "What do you want to be when you grow up?" Sophie held up her pencil. "A baseball player, right?"

"Maybe," said Toby. "Or maybe a reporter."

Sophie could feel her jaw drop. "Really? Me too!"

"Or maybe not," Toby said. He made a face and tilted his chair back. "My turn."

"Hang on!" Sophie said. She looked down at her paper. She still hadn't asked the last question she had added: Who is the most awesome person you know? It had been perfect for Kate, her best friend in the world. But Toby?

"Ask your dumb question already!" he groaned.

"Never mind," mumbled Sophie. "Go ahead."

Toby grinned. Of course he had made up very different questions. They included:

"What's your favorite football team?"

"What's your favorite baseball team?"

and

"Who's your favorite basketball player?"

Talk about dumb questions!

She answered, "Giants," to them all.

"There is no player named Giants," said Toby.

"Prove it," Sophie said.

"Whatever," Toby said back, slouching in his seat. "Okay. Last question. Do you have a nickname? Sophster? Sophmeister? Sophoraptor?" Toby laughed and put down his pencil. "Never mind. I know you don't."

Sophie looked at him. "Oh, yeah?" she said. She did too have a nickname. And it didn't sound like a dinosaur's name, either. "Sophie the Awesome!" she blurted.

She grinned with satisfaction. Then she noticed Toby's face. Before, it had looked grumpy. Now it looked like it would burst with laughter.

And then it did. Toby totally cracked up!

"Toby!" called Ms. Moffly from across the room. "Please lower your voice. And sit down!"

Oh, no, Sophie thought. This was not good. Not at all.

CHAPTER 9

Oh, no, no, no, no, no, no, no! What had Sophie done?

She had gone and put her precious new name in the grubby hands of Toby Myers. That was what!

She heard Ms. Moffly tell the class that their interview time was over. And she watched Toby go back to his desk and start laughing with Archie right away.

Of course he was making fun of her. Sophie could just tell. She wanted to scream! This was not at all how Sophie the Awesome was supposed to start!

Of course, it wouldn't have been so bad if she had set the jump-rope record. Or if she had done *anything* awesome so far that day. Then her awesomeness would have been proven. But Sophie could feel it in her guts. She should have waited till the next day to tell everyone her new name.

She had made a BIG mistake.

Maybe, if it was almost three o'clock, Ms. Moffly would let them wait and do their reports tomorrow. Sophie looked at the clock. It was only two-fifteen.

Sophie's stomach got all knotty as Ms. Moffly called the first group up.

"I interviewed Mindy," said Jack.

Mindy stood up and took a bow, and Lily applauded loudly.

"Anyway," Jack went on, "I asked her if she has any brothers and sisters. She doesn't. I asked her what her favorite sports are. She said gymnastics and ice-skating."

"And horseback riding!" Mindy added.

"You didn't say that," said Jack.

"I just remembered," said Mindy.

"And horseback riding," Jack repeated. "And I asked her how many teeth she lost. Six."

"That's all?" called out Archie. "I've lost eight."

The whole class giggled.

"I meant eight," said Mindy quickly. "Is it my turn now?"

"Yes, Mindy," said Ms. Moffly. "Thank you, Jack. And, class, please be respectful. You all know better than to interrupt."

The whole class nodded. That didn't stop the giggling, though.

There was giggling when Mindy said Jack had never had a dessert that was on fire before.

There was giggling when Grace said Ben's favorite cartoon character was Tweety Bird.

There was giggling when Eve said that Dean was afraid of butterflies.

There was even giggling when Sophie A. said that ants on a log were Kate's favorite snack. Sophie did not know what was so funny about that. Those things were good!

Sophie could only imagine how much giggling there would be when her nickname came up. It would ruin the whole name thing! Inside, her whole body groaned.

And then it was her turn.

"Sophie M.," said Ms. Moffly, "why don't you share with us now? And no more giggling, class, please."

Sophie looked at the clock. It was only two-forty. Could she make her report last twenty minutes? Long enough that Toby would have to wait till tomorrow? She would have to try.

"Sophie?" said Ms. Moffly. The teacher waited, then leaned toward her. "Sophie?" she said again.

There was giggling. Sophie pointed to herself and looked surprised.

"Huh? Who, me?" she said.

"Yes, you," said Ms. Moffly patiently.

"Oh, sorry." Sophie shrugged. "I thought you meant Sophie A."

"No," said Ms. Moffly. "I think I said 'Sophie

M.' And Sophie A. already went." She cut her eyes across the room. "No giggling, please!"

"So it's my turn?" said Sophie. She sighed and stood up with her paper.

She cleared her throat.

She counted to three.

Then four. Then five.

"Anytime, Sophie," said Ms. Moffly.

"Thank you," said Sophie. "Thank you very, very, very, very, very —"

"Sophie!" Ms. Moffly cut in.

"Much," Sophie said.

She breathed in. Then out. She looked around the classroom.

"Get on with it!" Archie yelled.

"Archie," Ms. Moffly said sharply. Then she turned back to Sophie. "It's okay to be nervous, Sophie. That's not usually like you," she added. "But please, just relax and go on."

Relax. Right. Sophie would do that. She would relax. And go slow.

"Okay...sooooo...I interviewed Toby. Toby Myers. You all know Toby, right?"

"Yes!" the class yelled.

Sophie cleared her throat again. "Okay. Sooooo...I interviewed Toby. Aaaand..."

Sophie carefully studied her paper. Then she picked at some green paint on the back of her hand.

"Yes?" said Ms. Moffly.

Sophie looked at the teacher. "And I found out what his favorite color is."

"Yes?" said Ms. Moffly again.

Sophie cleared her throat one more time. "Toby Myers' favorite color is...not blue," she said.

Giggles popped up all around the room. But Sophie didn't care. The longer it took for her to give her report, the better.

It was two forty-five. She just had to make her report last fifteen more minutes.

"That's enough, class," said Ms. Moffly. "Sophie, *please* go ahead."

"Toby . . . Myers' . . . favorite . . . color . . . iissssssss . . ." Sophie put a long pause between each word.

"Red!" Toby yelled.

The whole class clapped and cheered.

"And my favorite ice cream is chocolate! And I have two cats! And I want to be a reporter or a baseball player!" he added.

"Toby!" said Ms. Moffly.

"Sorry." He shrugged. "She was just going so slow. I was trying to help."

Help? Sophie glared at Toby harder than she'd ever glared before. She could feel laser beams shoot from her eyes. Well, almost. If they really had, that would have been awesome!

"I'm very sorry you were interrupted, Sophie," said Ms. Moffly. "Is there anything else you'd like to tell us?"

There sure was! Sophie wanted to tell everybody that Toby Myers was a big, giant pain in the neck! She wanted to tell them not to listen to anything else he had to say. She wanted to tell them that no matter how hard he and the whole class laughed at her that day, the next day she *would* earn her awesome new name.

But she didn't. She just said, "No," sat back down, and waited for Toby to ruin her life.

"I interviewed *her*," Toby said. He pointed a thumb in Sophie's direction.

"The name's Sophie Miller," Sophie muttered.

Everyone laughed.

Toby snuck Sophie a teasing look. He was thinking about her nickname. She just knew it. He was thinking about how he should say it, to make it sound as silly as he could.

Sophie put her head down on her desk.

Why did Toby have to be her partner?

And why did she have to tell him, of all people, her awesome new name?

Why couldn't she have kept her big mouth shut until the next day?

She did not feel like Sophie the Awesome. She felt like Sophie the Dumbest Girl in the Whole World.

"Anyway," Toby went on. "I found out that she says her favorite baseball and football teams are the Giants. But she probably doesn't have a clue, because that's just really weird."

"It's crazy!" yelled Archie.

"Archie! Toby!" Ms. Moffly said.

"Well, it is," Toby said. "And she says her favorite basketball player is a giant. I mean, they're tall. But giants? Come on."

He laughed, and a bunch of the boys joined him.

"That's enough," said Ms. Moffly. "And remember, Toby, your job as a reporter is to stick to the *facts*. Are there any other *facts* you'd like to add?"

Toby looked at Sophie.

Her face felt red. She could only imagine what it looked like. She waited for him to say her new name, and for the whole class to laugh. Again.

But Toby just shrugged and went back to his seat. "Nah. Nothin' else. She's way too boring," he said.

Of course, everyone started giggling. Everyone except Sophie. She had never been so happy to be called boring in her whole life!

Had Toby really just finished his report without making fun of the name Sophie the Awesome at all?

Sophie pinched herself. *Ouch!* Okay, she wasn't dreaming.

She didn't look at Toby, just in case it might remind him. But she silently thanked him. Who would have thought that Toby could do something so . . . awesome?

CHAPTER 10

The next thing Sophie knew, school was over. And she was glad. It had been a long day! She didn't know what had stopped Toby from making fun of her name in class, but it worried her. He could still change his mind and ruin everything. Any minute!

And if he didn't? What then? Did Sophie really have to thank him?

Ugh! That might be worse.

Sophie grabbed her backpack. She just wanted to get on the bus as soon as possible. Then she could start making plans with Kate for the next day—the day when she'd finally prove her awesomeness!

On the bus, Sophie pulled Kate to their favorite seat in the back row. Then she scrunched down, hoping that Ella wouldn't see her.

Ella Fitzgibbon was in kindergarten. She lived next door to Sophie...and she never left Sophie alone.

"*SOOOO*-PHIE!"

Her squeaky voice was getting closer.

"There you are!" Ella plopped down in the seat across from Kate and Sophie. Then she scrunched down, just like them. "Who are we hiding from?" she asked.

"No one." Sophie sighed. But Kate giggled. For some reason, she seemed to think Ella was cute. Sophie wondered if Kate would feel the same if Ella stuck to *her* like glue.

"Hey, what's in the box?" Kate asked.

Ella held up a boot-sized shoe box with crayon writing on it. Sophie read the scribbly letters. They spelled: ELLAS SLIИKYS. Huh?

"It's my Slinky collection!" said Ella as the bus pulled away from the school. "I brought it in for show-and-tell. I have twenty. And a half. Want to see?" she asked.

"Sure," said Kate. "Cool!"

"Kate!" Sophie whispered before Ella's box was opened. "We have things to discuss." She turned Kate's shoulders toward her. "Ella, you'll have to excuse us," she said.

But Kate looked puzzled. "What do we have to discuss?"

Sophie sighed. "'Sophie the Awesome.' Remember?" she whispered.

"Oh, right," Kate said. "But I thought you were just going to jump rope tomorrow."

"Yes," said Sophie. "But I was thinking, if we go out to the yard in the morning, I could try then, before school even begins. Then I can *start* the day as Sophie the Awesome!" *Before Toby can say anything to anybody*, she added silently to herself.

Kate thought for a second. Then she nodded. "Sounds good to me."

"Sounds good to me, too!" said Ella. She was leaning across the aisle, grinning. "What are you talking about, anyway?"

"Nothing," grumbled Sophie.

"What do you mean, 'nothing'?" Kate said. "We're talking about breaking the all-time jump-rope record! That's something, isn't it?"

Sophie had to admit that Kate had a point.

"Wow! That's awesome!" Ella said. "What's the record?"

Sophie got very serious. "One hundred and thirty-four," she said.

"Wow!" exclaimed Ella. "ONE HUNDRED AND THIRTY-FOUR!"

Everyone on the bus turned around.

"No yelling on the bus!" called Mrs. Blatt, the driver.

"Wow!" Ella whispered loudly. "That is a lot!"

Maybe Ella wasn't so bad after all.

That was when Sophie's big sister, Hayley, spoke up.

Hayley didn't speak to Sophie all that much.

She was in fifth grade and usually too busy doing something else.

On the bus, she was usually whispering with her friend Kim.

In school, she was usually following the boy she liked, Sam.

After school, she was usually at ballet class or at Kim's house.

And at home, she was usually on the computer or on the phone talking to Kim about Sam... or ballet... or... that was about it.

That left Sophie to keep Max, their two-year-old brother, out of trouble. But that was a whole other story!

"What's 'one hundred and thirty-four,' Ella?" Hayley asked, turning around in her seat a few rows up.

"It's the all-time jump-rope record!" said Ella proudly. "Sophie's going to break it. And I'm going to help her! Isn't that awesome?"

Sophie couldn't help it: She patted Ella on the

head. Ella was a pest, but she sure knew what to say.

Hayley, meanwhile, turned to Kim. They shared a we-know-everything-and-they-know-nothing look. Sophie knew it very well.

"That's not the record," Hayley said.

Sophie felt her heart skip. "It's not?" she asked.

"No!" said Kim. "Jenny Brown, in our class, has gone way over a thousand. She sets a new record, like, every day."

Sophie could feel every drop of awesomeness in her body draining away.

"I didn't know that," she whispered to Kate. "Did you?"

Kate shook her head.

"It's probably because you're just in the third grade," said Hayley. "But it's true. That's the all-time record. I mean, I guess you could try to break it." She laughed. "But no one has ever even come close."

Then Hayley and Kim turned around and started whispering again.

Sophie leaned against the seat in front of her. "A thousand jumps? I can never beat that!" she moaned.

"Sure you can!" said Ella. She grinned at her. "You can do anything, Sophie!"

But Sophie wasn't sure. Being awesome was turning out to be a lot harder than she'd thought!

"Hey, knock-knock," said Kate.

"Not now," sighed Sophie.

"Who's there?" Ella said.

"Yukon," said Kate.

"Yukon who?" asked Ella.

"Yukon do it, Sophie!" Kate said. She gave Sophie a quick hug. "Here's our stop!"

The bus breaks hissed and the door folded open. The kids from Sophie's stop began to unload.

"Come on, Soph," said Kate. "How about you come over to my house and we make a new plan?"

Sophie nodded. "Okay," she said glumly.

"Can I come, too?" asked Ella, climbing down the steps behind them.

"I don't think so, Ella," Sophie said. Making big plans like this was no job for kindergartners. "This is too important."

The bus roared away, and Sophie and Kate started up the hill to Kate's house. Sophie could hear Ella behind them.

"Wait for me!" Ella cried. "It's hard to run with all these—Oh, no! *My Slinkys!*"

Sophie whirled around to see Ella standing on the sidewalk. She was holding an empty box. And she was watching with wide, wide eyes as all twenty and a half Slinkys slinked down the street.

"My Slinkys!" Ella cried again. And she started running... right toward the road!

Sophie didn't even stop to think.

"No, Ella!" she cried. "Stay out of the street!"

She ran as fast as she could after her. Then she lunged for Ella's backpack and caught it by the

strap. She gave it a hard yank. But Ella's backpack slipped right off her shoulders!

"Ella!" Sophie cried again.

She reached out and grabbed Ella's shirt. And this time, she pulled even harder.

And this time, Ella stopped, her toes right at the edge of the curb.

The very next second, a car whizzed past them.

"Whoa!" said Ella.

"Wow!" said all the other kids from their bus stop, who had run up. "That was close!"

Sophie took a deep breath. Yes, it was!

Suddenly, Ella turned around and hugged Sophie's stomach. Hard!

"Sophie, you're my hero!" she exclaimed.

Sophie looked down at Ella's sandy-colored head. She winced as Ella squeezed even harder.

"Easy, Ella!" gasped Sophie. "That hurts. Besides, I didn't really do anything."

She tried to pry Ella off. But the kindergartner wasn't budging.

"Yes, you did!" said Ella. "You saved my life!"

"You really did," said Kate.

Slowly, Ella turned her head to peer down the street. "It's just too bad you couldn't save my Slinkys...."

Sophie looked down the street, too. She watched the Slinkys tumble on. They looked like an army of wild, rainbow-colored macaronis.

Then the car that had driven by them stopped at the bottom of the hill. The door opened, and their neighbor, old Mrs. Dixon, jumped out. She began to scoop up all the Slinkys.

"Yay, Mrs. Dixon!" shouted Ella. "Don't forget the pink one!"

Ella finally let go of Sophie. Whew. Sophie could breathe again. But she still had a tight, warm feeling in her stomach. Sophie could not help but grin. It was a good feeling!

"You know what this means?" said Kate. She grabbed Sophie's hands and swung them. "It means...knock-knock!"

"Who's there?" said Sophie.

"the," said Kate.

"Sophie the who?" said Sophie.

"Sophie the Awesome!" said Kate.

Sophie had to laugh. But then she shook her head.

"No?" said Kate.

"No," said Sophie.

Saving Ella's life was definitely name-worthy. But Sophie had an even more awesome name than "Awesome" now. A name that, she hoped, was a little easier to prove, too.

She put her hands on her hips and stuck out her chin. "It's Sophie the *Hero,* that's who!"

So maybe SOPHIE the AWESOME isn't the perfect name.

But SOPHIE the HERO might be!

Take a peek at Sophie's next adventure....

Kate left Sophie in the hall and stepped into Room 10.

"Ladies and gentlemen! And everyone else, too," Kate declared. (Sophie bet she was talking to yucky Toby Myers and Archie Dolan.) "May I have your attention, please?"

Sophie heard the class get quiet, no kidding. Wow! How lucky was she to have Kate for a sidekick? Kate was very good at this!

"What is it?" someone said.

That's when Kate grabbed Sophie and pulled her into the room.

"I'd like you to meet the one, the only . . . Sophie the Hero!" Kate cried.

"Sophie the who?"

"Sophie the what?"

Sophie took a bow and cleared her throat. "Sophie the Hero," she said.

And just as Sophie had hoped, she and Kate got to tell the Slinky story all over again.

And again!

"Wow! You are a hero!" said Eve, Mia, Sydney, and Grace when it was over.

"I am happy to sign autographs," Sophie said. "Does anyone have a pen?"

"Wait a minute," said a snooty voice. It belonged to Mindy VonBoffmann. Her name would have been Mindy the Meanie, if Sophie had anything to say about it.

"What happened to the Slinkys?" Mindy asked.

Sophie shrugged. "Mrs. Dixon picked them up."

"Then isn't *she* the real hero?" Mindy said. She crossed her arms and made a face that Sophie's mom would have called sassy.

"Yeah," Lily Lemley chimed in. She liked to copy Mindy, so she made her face look just the same. "If Mrs. Dixon saved the Slinkys, she's the real hero," Lily said.

"What are you talking about?" Kate said. "Sophie saved a kindergartner! Who cares about the Slinkys?"

"They only cost a dollar or something," Ben added. "Kindergartners cost a lot more."

Good old Ben. Sophie turned to smile at him.

She truly felt like a hero. And that felt really good!

But Mindy just shrugged. "I guess," she said. "Still, it's only one kindergartner. It's not like she saved five kittens from a burning building, like Scarlett the cat. Remember? Now that's a real hero."

"Yeah, that's a real hero," Lily echoed.

Sophie remembered the story their second grade teacher, Mrs. Cruz, had read to them the year before. It was a true story about a stray cat who saved the lives of all her kittens. When the building they lived in caught fire, she carried them out, one by one.

Okay. Yes. Sophie knew the cat was a real hero. But she was, too!

Before Sophie could say anything, Toby Myers spoke up. "You don't know what you're talking about," he told Mindy.

Sophie's mouth dropped open. She could not believe it. *Was* Toby *standing up for her?*

Until last year, this would not have surprised Sophie. Until last year, she and Toby had been best friends. But things changed in second grade. Toby started hanging out with Archie Dolan, and Kate moved to town. Now Sophie and Kate were best friends. And Sophie and Toby could not look at each other.

If they did, they had to stick out their tongues.

But maybe things were changing. . . .

Sophie thought of the day before, when Toby had actually done something *nice* for her. He had not made fun of that day's name—Sophie the Awesome—at all.

Was it possible? Could Toby actually be coming to his senses?

"*Real* heroes save the world from evil aliens and giant asteroids and killer robots!" Toby said. Then he looked at Sophie and stuck out his tongue.

No. Sophie sighed. She guessed he had not changed, after all.

"Yeah!" said Archie. "And heroes have a mutant power." He pointed at Sophie with a sticky, stubby finger. "What's your mutant power, Sophie?" he asked.

Toby held his nose. "Super BO!" He laughed.

"Not funny," Kate said.

But Sophie just rolled her eyes—and secretly sniffed her armpit, just to be sure.

No, she did not have BO. And, yes, no matter what Toby or Archie or Mindy said, Sophie was a hero.

She stuck her own tongue out at Toby.

So there!

SO MANY PERFECT PUPPIES – COLLECT THEM ALL!